for

THORA HOWELL

who said to Eugenie,

"Here comes somebody

you should meet,"

as Maria paddled up to

the dock in her kayak.

Thank you, Thora,

for sparking the friendship

that led to this book.

M.C. & E.F.

We acknowledge the support of the Canada Council for the Arts,
the Ontario Arts Council, and the Government of Canada through
the Book Publishing Industry Development Program (BPIDP)
for our publishing activities.

Cataloging in Publication Data
Coffey, Maria, 1952-
A cat in a kayak

ISBN 1-55037-509-1 (bound) ISBN 1-55037-508-3 (pbk.)

I. Fernandes, Eugenie, 1943- . II. Title.

PS8555.033C27 1998   jC813'.54   C97-931680-4
PZ7.C6485Ca 1998

The art in this book was rendered in gouache.
The text was typeset in Seagull.

Distributed in Canada by:
Firefly Books Ltd.
3680 Victoria Park Avenue, Willowdale, ON M2H 3K1

Published in the U.S.A. by Annick Press (U.S.) Ltd.
Distributed in the U.S.A. by:
Firefly Books (U.S.) Inc.
P.O. Box 1338, Ellicott Station, Buffalo, NY 14205

Printed and bound in Canada by
Friesens, Altona, Manitoba.

visit us at: **www.annickpress.com**

A Cat in a Kayak

Story • Maria Coffey
Art • Eugenie Fernandes

Annick Press Ltd.
Toronto • New York • Vancouver

Mrs. Pickles went to see Victor the vet with a huge, fluffy cat in her arms. "The janitor of my apartment building has put up a 'No Pets' sign," she told him, wiping away a tear. "He says Teelo has to go."

"Don't worry, Mrs. Pickles," said Victor kindly. "I love cats and Cloud Island has no janitors, so Teelo can live there with me."

That evening, Victor carried Teelo down to the city dock. He pointed across the harbour, towards a little island that seemed to float above the ocean.

"There's your new home, Teelo," he said.

Teelo's eyes grew big and round as Victor carried him past the sturdy fishing boats and tug boats and up to something that was small and skinny and shaped like a banana split.

"Here's our kayak," said Victor. He slid the kayak into the water, clambered into the cockpit with Teelo round his neck and paddled away.

The kayak danced about in the waves, and the wind whistled by, dousing Teelo with spray. He dug his claws into Victor's life jacket and shut his eyes tight. He kept them shut until the bow of the kayak scraped against the shore and he heard Victor say, "Welcome to Cloud Island, Teelo."

Opening his eyes at last, Teelo saw a smooth, shining beach, a tall green forest and a snug wooden house with flowers spilling from its window boxes.

Teelo's new home was quiet and peaceful and he was happy there. Every morning before breakfast, he did yoga in the kitchen with Victor, bending and stretching and breathing deeply. When Victor paddled off to the city in his kayak, Teelo curled up under the wood stove, snoozing happily. Things just couldn't have been better, until...

...Victor came home with Ruby the rooster and three hens in the cockpit of his kayak.

"Mr. Batty's neighbours complained about the noise they made," he explained to Teelo. "I think they're such cheerful birds, and we don't have any neighbours for them to disturb, so I told Mr. Batty that they could live with us."

Teelo thought the birds were a nuisance. Ruby was a show-off who crowed all day and danced flamenco in the kitchen, flapping his wings and stamping his claws. The hens clucked and pecked at Teelo's food, and when he went for a snooze he found they'd laid a pile of brown eggs in his favourite spot under the wood stove.

So Teelo found a new spot to snooze, on the window seat, out of the way of Ruby the rooster and the hens. And things were fine, until...

...Victor came home with Terry the terrier in the back hatch of his kayak.

"Mrs. Gripe couldn't keep Terry anymore because he ruined her curtains," he explained. "I think he's such a friendly dog, and we don't have any curtains for him to destroy, so I told Mrs. Gripe that Terry could live with us."

Teelo thought Terry was a pain. He barked all day, and ran around the kitchen, picking up towels and rugs and books and newspapers and shaking them to bits. And when Teelo went for a snooze on the window seat, he found Terry there, ripping up the cushion. So Teelo found a new spot to snooze, on top of the fridge, out of the way of Ruby the rooster, the hens and Terry the terrier. And things were bearable, until...

...Victor came home with Sylvie the snake wrapped round the bow of his kayak.

"Sylvie grew too long for Mr. Punk's apartment," he explained. "I think she's such an elegant snake, and we've got lots of room, so I told Mr. Punk that Sylvie could live with us."

Teelo thought Sylvie was spooky. She sashayed up the lamp stand, and draped herself over the pictures on the walls. She slithered right out of her old skin and left it lying all over the kitchen floor. And when Teelo went for a snooze on the top of the fridge, he found Sylvie there, waiting to give him a friendly squeeze. So Teelo found a new spot to snooze, up on the roof of the house, out of the way of Ruby the rooster, the hens, Terry the terrier and Sylvie the snake. And things were just about tolerable, until...

...Victor came home with Bonaparte the parrot on his head.

"Bonaparte got much too bossy for Colonel Pond's wife," Victor explained. "I think he's a hilarious parrot, and I don't have a wife for him to upset, so I told Colonel Pond that Bonaparte could live with us."

Teelo thought Bonaparte was appalling. He stood on his perch in the kitchen shrieking orders at everyone.

"Atten-tion! At ease! Hup, two, three, four, hup, two, three, four, hup, two, three, four! MARCH!"

When Teelo went for a snooze on the roof, Bonaparte flew up after him. He stomped up and down the gable, yelling, "Rise and SHINE! Rise and SHINE! Atten-TION!"

THINGS WERE IMPOSSIBLE! Teelo couldn't bear being around any of these crazy creatures a moment longer! He left the house, went into the forest and climbed a tree. From his hiding place amid its branches he watched the other animals greeting Victor when he came home: Sylvie the snake hissed happily, Terry the terrier tugged at Victor's pant leg, growling with glee, and the rooster, the hens and the parrot perched on Victor's head and shoulders, crowing and clucking and shrieking with joy.

"What a noisy lot you are!" Victor teased them. "Tomorrow's my day off; I'm going to Thunder Rock in my kayak to find some peace and quiet!"

Teelo's ears pricked up. Peace and quiet? That's what he was longing for!

When darkness descended, Teelo climbed out of the tree, crept down to the beach and stowed away in Victor's kayak. He thought happily of all the peace and quiet he would find on Thunder Rock. But when he fell asleep, he dreamed he was out at sea in a little boat, being rolled about by the waves and drenched with spray. Suddenly he woke up—and this wasn't a dream at all!

He *was* at sea, in Victor's kayak, and the waves were high and steep, with curling white crests! Sticking his head out of the hatch, he looked about. Behind him, Cloud Island had shrunk to a tiny dot; ahead, a dark, forbidding island was looming up. He meowed fearfully, and Victor turned around, astonished to find that he had a cat in his kayak.

"Teelo!" he cried. "You adventurous fellow!"

Teelo wasn't feeling adventurous—he just wanted
some peace and quiet. But as Victor paddled towards
Thunder Rock, things got less and less peaceful and
more and more noisy and chaotic. Waves smashed
against the cliffs. Hundreds of sea birds wheeled
about, deafening Teelo with their screaming and

screeching. Scores of seals bobbed up, and flocks of
honking geese skimmed past. Suddenly, right next to the
kayak, a pod of killer whales surfaced; they spy-hopped
and breached with terrific splashes, and fixed Teelo with
their beady black eyes.

Teelo was terrified, and he couldn't wait to get to land.

On Thunder Rock, however, things were even worse. Huge sea lions with long yellow fangs came lumbering down the beach. They barked furiously at Teelo, opening their bristly mouths wide and sending clouds of steam high into the air. As he ran away from them, a shadow loomed over Teelo and a bald eagle swooped down and tried to grab him in its talons.

When he dived for cover behind a rock, a big red crab threatened him with its sharp pincers. And as he fled back towards the kayak, an octopus in a tidal pool reached out a tentacle and tugged his tail.

Teelo was so glad to leave Thunder Rock that he didn't mind when the waves grew bigger than ever, tossing the kayak about, or when the wind gusted hard, drenching him with spray. He hung on tight as Victor paddled back to Cloud Island, and soon he saw the smooth shining beach, the tall green forest and the snug little house with flowers spilling from its window boxes.

Inside the house, Ruby the rooster was crowing and dancing flamenco, the hens were clucking and laying eggs, Terry the terrier was barking and tearing up cushions, Sylvie the snake was hissing and Bonaparte the parrot was bossing everyone about...

...but Teelo didn't mind in the least. He stretched out happily on the kitchen floor among all the other animals, thinking what a friendly place this was after Thunder Rock, and how very glad he was to be home.